Piko the Penguinaut

by M. K. Abraham
Illustrated by R. R. Jan

STORYROBINBOOKS

California, USA

Description:

Piko the penguin wants to go into space, and he believes he's found a simple way to get there. But it's not as easy as he thinks. As problems mount, Piko realizes he'll need the help of his friends. They must work together and use all their creativity to outwit foes and solve problems. Only then can Piko hope to realize his outer space dream.

In this story, children learn the values of problem solving, collaboration, and creativity along with the importance of critical thinking and wise decision making.

ISBN 978-1-937489-00-7

Library of Congress Control Number: 2011934055

StoryRobin Books
P. O. Box 2247
Sunnyvale, CA 94087
www.storyrobin.com

Printed and bound in China

M. K. Abraham: *To Marilyn, for all her ethereal goodness and motherly devotion.*

R. R. Jan: *To my family, Phoebe for her constant support, my rabbit (for he is always by my side while I am working), and all my friends.*

Table of Contents

Group Picture

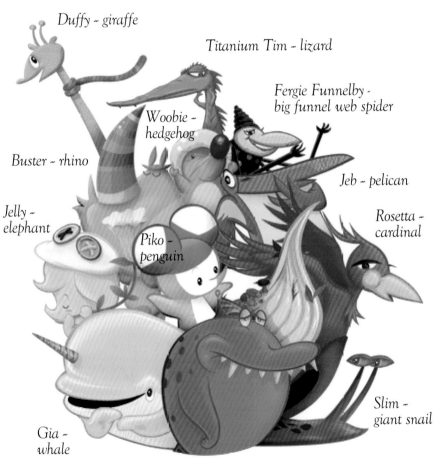

Duffy ~ giraffe

Titanium Tim ~ lizard

Fergie Funnelby ~
big funnel web spider

Woobie ~
hedgehog

Buster ~ rhino

Jeb ~ pelican

Jelly ~
elephant

Rosetta ~
cardinal

Piko ~
penguin

Slim ~
giant snail

Gia ~
whale

The Blue Grumble ~ troll

Chapter 1

What's Wrong
with Golly Geyser?

Piko the penguin stepped out of his toadstool hut and stretched his stubby little wings and wiggled his stubby little tail. He had just finished a dinner of sardines, and his stomach was full. This was his favorite time of day. The trees and flowers had a golden glow about them. Birds were in full song, frogs were burping, and butterflies fluttered everywhere. Off in the distance he spotted Duffy the giraffe. Her head was just visible above the trees. She was looking at something, her ears alert. Sometimes Piko wished he were a giraffe so he could see over everything. Duffy was so tall she could see most of Robin Island.

Piko brushed some fallen leaves from his doorstep, then washed his beak and wingtips in a stump basin. As he was wiping his beak dry on a squeak bush, he noticed that Duffy hadn't moved. He walked over to her.

"What's up, Duffy?" he asked. "Is something wrong?"

"I haven't seen Golly Geyser yet," she answered. "It's overdue. It should shoot high into the sky every day about this time. But I haven't seen it."

"Maybe it's tired and is sleeping in."

"But geysers don't sleep."

"Maybe we should go take a look," Piko said.

As they headed toward the geyser, they saw Woobie the hedgehog struggling to straighten his gourd house. It must have shifted again. Piko thought he should prop it up better, but he never did.

Woobie grunted when Piko and Duffy greeted him. Then he asked, "What are you up to?"

"Something's wrong with Golly Geyser. It hasn't gone off all day."

"All day? No, no, that's not right. It should shoot into the sky every three hours. Every three hours. Always."

Woobie gave his gourd house a final nudge, then joined them. Behind him, his gourd house shifted once more.

Near the center of the village they came to a big black stump. They called it Crazy Stump because of the stubby trunks and branches rising from it. Jelly the elephant leaned against Crazy Stump, rubbing her back. Dozing on top of her massive head was Jeb the pelican.

"Is there food?" squawked Jeb, waking up as they approached. "Are you headed for a feast?"

"All you can think of is food," said Jelly. "What's up, Piko?"

After Piko explained about Golly Geyser, Jelly lifted the tip of her trunk to scratch her head. "That can't be right." She took one of her giant steps and joined them.

"Hey!" Jeb squawked and flapped his wings, almost falling off the elephant's head. "Well, I guess I might as well ride along."

As Piko, Duffy, Woobie, Jelly, and Jeb neared Golly Geyser, they met Buster the rhinoceros.

"Hi, Buster," said Piko. "We're here to check on Golly Geyser. Do you know why it's been so quiet?"

Buster's tiny eyes sparkled. "Look!" he said, stepping aside so they could see. "I pushed a big rock onto Golly Geyser! See? See? I did that. A big rock. I pushed it onto the geyser."

They all looked in alarm at the big rock on top of Golly Geyser. Duffy the giraffe lowered her long neck and put her face right in front of Buster. "Why? Why did you do that?"

"I don't know. To see what happens. Only nothing's happened. Nothing. Did I kill Golly Geyser?"

"When did you do this?" asked Piko.

"Do what?"

"Put the rock on the geyser!" exclaimed Piko.

"Oh, this morning, just after the sun came up."

They heard a rumbling.

"This isn't good," said Piko. "We should ask Rosetta what to do." But before he could say more, the ground began to shake.

"Run!" shouted Duffy.

But no one could run because the ground was shaking too much. Then with a boom the big rock shot into the sky on a fountain of water as Golly Geyser geysered like never before.

"Wow!" they cried together, watching the big rock sail upward, getting smaller and smaller until it disappeared from sight.

"See?" said Buster. "Now I know. I know what happens when I put a big rock on Golly Geyser."

The geyser slowly tapered off. Piko grew uneasy.

"Everyone," he said. "Have you ever heard the saying, 'What goes up, must come down?'"

"Yeah, I've heard that before," said Duffy.

"Me, too," echoed the other animals.

All of them looked straight up.

"Eek!" cried Buster, taking tiny but heavy steps all about, which shook the ground almost as much as the geyser had. "Eek!"

"Run for cover!" cried Piko. "That cave! Run for that cave!"

Piko and Woobie dashed into the nearby cave, and Jeb flew in after them. But Duffy the giraffe, Jelly the elephant, and Buster the rhino were too big to fit. "What'll we do!" they cried.

Piko looked at Duffy's scarf tied high around her neck. It was blowing in the breeze. "The wind's blowing that way, so that's where the rock will probably fall. Run the other way! Run!"

Soon Duffy, Jelly, and Buster had run from sight.

Piko hoped he was right. He didn't know for sure where the rock might land. But suddenly Buster came lumbering back.

"Why did you come back?" asked Piko.

"I got lost," said Buster.

"How can you get lost?" asked Duffy. "You live around here!"

"I'm too nervous to think!" Buster looked up again. "The sky is falling! The sky is falling!"

"Not the sky," said Woobie. "Just that big rock you put on the geyser!"

"Buster, stand straight and tall," said Piko. "Be as thin as you can be."

"Why?"

"To be a smaller target!"

Buster did his best, but he couldn't really be thin.

They waited and they waited. Nothing happened. Then Duffy and Jelly came back. They waited some more. Still nothing happened.

"Shouldn't it have fallen by now?" asked Jelly.

Piko stepped out of the cave and peeked up. Woobie and Jeb followed. "Maybe it went all the way up."

"All the way up?" asked Duffy. "What do you mean by that?"

"Into space," said Piko. "I think it went all the way into outer space."

Chapter 2

Piko's Big Idea

That night, Piko couldn't sleep. He tossed and turned in his hammock just outside his hut. He kept looking up at the twinkling stars in the night sky. Wouldn't it be wonderful to go up into space? Maybe he could. Maybe he could go up into space the same way that rock did. But what would it take? He certainly couldn't just sit down on that geyser. He'd be boiled alive. And up there in space, he would need air.

He needed to talk to Rosetta the cardinal. She was the wisest animal on the island. Even though it was nighttime, he walked all the way to Rosetta's night roost. It was a dead tree whose bark had turned white. Although it was lifeless, Rosetta's home always sprouted flowers.

"Rosetta," Piko called softly. "Rosetta."

Finally a sleepy-eyed Rosetta peeked out of a hollow near the top. Her red crest was crooked, and her red feathers were ruffled. When she saw Piko, she did not look pleased.

"Do you realize what time it is?" Rosetta said.

Piko apologized, but then burst out with his idea of going into space. He explained how Buster had plugged the geyser with a rock, and when the geyser finally went off, it sent the rock into space.

"I could launch myself the same way, couldn't I? If I could somehow not get burned from the geyser's hot water?"

"So that's the racket I heard yesterday," said Rosetta. "Yes, I suppose if you had an airtight container, it might work."

"I knew it!" cried Piko. "I'm going into space!"

"Piko," said Rosetta as she became more fully awake, "there's more to it than just an airtight container. You need to think this all out carefully. Know

everything you need before you start. Because if you forget something, you may have to start all over."

"I won't forget anything. I won't."

Rosetta sighed. "Piko. This is bigger than you. You're going to need help. You need a team."

It was Piko's turn to sigh. "That will just slow things down!"

"Talk to your friends tomorrow," Rosetta said. "I'm sure they'll help you. Then go see Slim the snail."

"Slim? But he's the slowest thing on this island!" Piko grumbled, wishing he hadn't told Rosetta of his idea.

"Still, he's very good at organizing things. You talk to Slim about the project, okay?" Rosetta yawned. "Now please, I really need to get some sleep if I'm to catch that early worm."

Chapter 3

Slim the Snail

The next morning, Piko went to see his friends. Soon he had rounded up Duffy the giraffe, Woobie the hedgehog, Jelly the elephant, Jeb the pelican, and Buster the rhino. He told them what he wanted to do and asked if they would help.

"Of course we'll help," said Duffy, looking down from her tall neck. "That's what friends are for."

The others agreed as well.

"I promised Rosetta we'd include Slim the snail in this," Piko said.

"Slim!" said Buster, shaking his rhinoceros horn. "But all he can do is crawl. And he can barely do that! He's so slow."

Piko sighed. "I know. Still, he's very good at organizing things."

It wasn't hard to track down Slim. They just followed his slime trail. Soon they spotted his big spiral shell under a mossy tree. They gathered around him.

"All right, all right," said Slim, his eyestalks weaving to take them in. "I know this isn't a social visit. I'm not the most interesting guy. So what's up?"

"No one can organize a project better than you," said Piko.

"Just as I thought. That's the only reason anyone visits me. Okay, what do you want to do? No details yet. Just the basic idea."

Duffy lowered her head from above the trees and leaned in close to the snail's pudgy face. "We want to put someone into outer space."

"Put someone into space. Like a rocket or a spaceship? Sure, we can do that. We'll need a bigger team, though — a team of a few thousand. They have to be smart. Very, very smart and willing to work hard. They won't work for free, so we'll have to pay them somehow. If we can manage all that, I'm sure we can put someone into space in about 20 years."

"What!" cried everyone.

"We'll have to design a rocket engine," explained Slim, "and then come up with a formula for the fuel. We'll need to build a spaceship. We'll need to build a launching pad—" Slim paused. "Is something the matter?"

Piko felt overwhelmed. "We thought maybe we could just use Golly Geyser." He then explained how Buster had plugged the geyser with a rock, and when the geyser finally went off, it sent the rock into space.

Slim thought about this. "Hmmm. Yes, that could work. That makes things a lot simpler. Still, there are things to consider. First off, we'll need an airtight container."

"A spaceship!" cried Piko. "We'll call it Star Racer!"

"More like a tin can," said Slim. But seeing how Piko didn't like hearing it called that, he added, "Fine, Star Racer. But we'll need a way to keep it cool while it sits on the geyser. And after it's up there in space, how do we make it come down? As for the landing, it has to be soft, so we'll need a parachute. And what about air? Will the ship have enough air?"

Piko began to realize just how big a project this really was.

"Then there's the hardest part of all," said Slim. "Finding a pilot. We're going to have to find some idiot to go up in the thing."

Everyone fell silent. Finally Piko stepped forward. "That would be me."

Slim's eyestalks twitched in alarm.Then he straightened them, pretending not to be concerned. "Okay, that's settled.

Now, let's keep this meeting short because I need to get somewhere. Woobie, can you handle the business side of this?"

"Yes!" cried Woobie the hedgehog, pulling out a notebook. "I'll keep track of everything! I'll write down all the assignments and make sure people do what they're supposed to do. If we make any deals, if we trade things, I'll keep track of that, too!"

"Good," said Slim. "Everyone, keep Woobie informed about what you're doing and every deal you make. We don't want any surprises when it comes time to launch."

"We should have a project fund," said Woobie, jotting in his notebook, "to cover expenses. Everyone, give me your pearls."

"Our pearls!" exclaimed Jelly. "Why should we give you our pearls?"

"Yeah," said Duffy. "Our pearls belong to us, not you."

"Don't worry," said Woobie. "You'll get them back when we're done. In fact, you'll get more back than you put in! Right now we need pearls to pay for everything we need for the launch. In the end, we'll have more pearls than we started with."

Piko lifted a wingtip and scratched beneath his cap. "How exactly does that work?"

Woobie's whiskers curled upward as he smiled. "We'll charge admission to the launch."

"Excellent," said Slim. "We'll make everyone pay to see the idiot — uh, to see Piko — go up into space."

"We'll charge two pearls each to watch the launch," said Woobie. "That will get us lots of pearls, you'll see."

"If anyone comes to watch," said Buster.

"They will if we tell them about it," said Jelly. "We need to tell the whole island." She raised her trunk in the air and trumpeted.

"The more who know, the more who'll come," agreed Woobie. "The more who come, the more pearls we'll get."

Slim looked slowly around at everyone. "So. What's it going to be?"

Everyone rounded up their pearls and gave them to Woobie.

"We're on our way," said Slim. "I'm setting the launch date for the end of the month. That will give us 29 days to prepare."

"29 days!" cried Piko. "Why so long? I'm sure we could be ready in a week."

"Things don't always go smoothly," said Slim. "You have to allow for surprises. We need some wiggle room for that."

Slim handed out assignments. Jeb would tell his pelican friends about the launch, and they would relay it to everyone on the island. Jelly and Buster would figure out a way to keep the spaceship cool while it sat on the geyser. Duffy would make a parachute for a soft landing. Woobie would keep track of the pearls and all the tasks.

As everyone went running off to start their assignments, Piko felt lost and left out. He had been given nothing to do to help. Soon he was the only one standing there. He looked up at the snail.

"Piko," said Slim. "We're going to need a spaceship."

Chapter 4

The Blue Grumble

As Piko wandered about, not knowing how to begin, Rosetta fluttered down to a nearby limb. "How's the project going?" she asked.

"Everyone's got tasks," he said. "They're making progress. But not me. I'm stuck. I'm supposed to build a spaceship, only I don't know how."

Rosetta thought about this. "Maybe you don't have to build one." She fluttered to an even closer limb. "You should pay the bog a visit."

"The bog?" Piko had heard terrible things about that place. "Why should I go there?"

"A lizard lives there. He's a hermit. I don't even know his name. But I've glimpsed things he's made — not a very good look, because he hates birds." Ruffling her feathers, Rosetta pointed with a wingtip to a bare spot on her stomach.

"The lizard did that?"

Rosetta nodded. "He's very good with a slingshot."

"But I'm a bird, too!" exclaimed Piko.

"Well, you're a flightless bird. You barely have wings at all. Just keep them tucked in, and he'll never notice."

Piko wasn't so sure about that.

"Anyway, I'm certain the lizard would have what you need. But you better be prepared to trade him something for it. Something he wants."

Piko wondered what a lizard might want. Fish! Since the lizard lived far from the ocean and any pond, he probably didn't get to eat fish often. Yes, that's what he would take him.

"Promise me one thing, Piko," said Rosetta. "When you do get your spaceship, test it in the ocean. Make sure it's airtight. Space is a very dangerous place. If there's a leak, you'll lose all your air. And without air, you won't be able to breathe. Promise me you'll test your spaceship in the ocean."

"I promise," said Piko.

Piko dove into the village pond and caught eight fish. Putting them in his backpack, he set off for the bog.

To get there, he knew he would have to cross Don't Look Down Gulch. He had never seen it before, but knew that there were only two ways across. One was by a bridge run by a troll called the Blue Grumble. The other through a long funnel web belonging to a spider named Fergie Funnelby. Piko decided to try the bridge since Fergie ate most everyone who entered her funnel web.

Don't Look Down Gulch was terrible to behold. Deeper than the highest island cliff, it had jagged rocks all the way down. Anyone who fell down there would never get out.

Walking along the edge of the gulch, Piko came to a sign that said "Bridge." But he didn't see a bridge. All he saw was a tall tree that curled outward over the gulch. The tree had a hollow in its base. As Piko stood there, puzzled, the Blue Grumble emerged from the hollow holding an abacus.

"Hi, Blue Grumble," Piko said. "I hear you have a wonderful bridge."

The troll nodded.

Piko waited, but the Blue Grumble said no more. "I'd like to cross your bridge. Would that be okay?"

The troll pointed to several buckets of blueberries stacked next to the tree.

"You like blueberries?" Piko asked.

The troll licked his very big and very blue lips and rubbed his stomach.

"If I picked you a bucketful, then would you let me cross your bridge?"

The Blue Grumble shook his head, then worked his abacus, pushing the beads back and forth, back and forth. "One," he said.

"One blueberry? All you want is one blueberry?"

The troll nodded, then added, "Next time two, after that four, so on, so on."

Wow, Piko thought. If the troll really did have a bridge, he could cross it a whole lot of times, and it still wouldn't amount to a bucketful. "Okay, a deal!" He dashed off, picked a blueberry from a nearby bush, and brought it back.

Taking the blueberry, the troll strolled over to the tree and kicked it hard. With a shudder, the tree uncoiled, stretching like a ribbon across the gulch. Soon it hung suspended from one side to the other, swaying gently in the breeze.

"Amazing!" exclaimed Piko, for it was a wonderful bridge. "Would you like a fish as well?" he asked, feeling guilty about paying so little. But the troll shook his huge head. Then Piko walked carefully across the swaying bridge, keeping his eyes straight ahead.

Chapter 5

Piko Meets the Lizard

As Piko traveled on, the landscape began to change. The trees grew short and gnarly, and moss hung from them like beards. Then the ground became spongy, and he knew he had reached the bog. Soon he began to smell something very rotten. At first he thought it was the bog. But then he realized it was his fish! This was much too long a journey to keep fish fresh. Sighing, he stopped and tossed all the fish into a swamp. Then he kept walking toward the center of the bog, because he had come too far to turn back now.

Around him, the trees became ever smaller and more twisted. Now he saw big, mossy shapes all about. Hearing a voice up ahead, he ducked behind one of the shapes, and peeked around it.

A lizard stood a short distance away. He was light green and dark green, covered in scales from snout to tail. Standing on his hind legs, he circled a very large root that stood up out of the bog. As he circled, he sang, and the root began to change shape. Then he shouted, and the shape froze. It was like a statue of a fish.

It was a wonderful fish — plump, pointed, with a hint of fins. Piko wanted to clap, but he dared not. Then the lizard turned sharply in his direction, his long tongue flicking out. "Sardines? Why do I smell sardines?" His beady eyes cast about. "Who's there?"

Piko knew there was no point in hiding from someone with such sharp senses. Tucking his wings tight to his sides, he stepped into view.

"Just me," he said.

The lizard ducked his head. "Who are you? Why are you here? Go away. I don't like visitors."

"My name's Piko," he said. "I don't mean you any harm. I came to talk to you. What were you doing just now?"

"Sculpting. I was sculpting. But you don't need to know that. Spies. Spies everywhere. Who do you work for? What are you after?"

"I don't work for anyone," said Piko. "And what would I be spying on? Do you really have so many secrets?"

The lizard seemed less sure of himself. "Well, no. But I might, someday." He puffed out his chest. "Someday I might have lots of secrets."

"Well, you've got one really big secret," said Piko. "And that's how good a sculptor you are! That was amazing, how you sculpted that root just now."

The lizard shrugged his shoulders. "It was nothing."

"Nothing? It was wonderful. What's your name?"

"Titanium Tim."

"Titanium Tim, master sculptor," said Piko. "I bet you could sculpt anything."

Titanium Tim shuffled his feet. "Not yuckmawlies," he murmured.

"Yuckmawlies?" repeated Piko, not liking the word at all.

The lizard clawed about in the bog and pulled something up. He tossed it over his shoulder to Piko. "That's a yuckmawly."

Piko caught it with a webbed foot, keeping his wings tucked. He studied it. The name fit because it was very ugly, like a squashed bug that was ugly before it got squashed, all wrinkled and covered in warts. "It's got lots of pretty colors," Piko said, trying to say something positive about it.

"But the shape is ugly," said Titanium Tim. "And it can't be sculpted. Here, watch this." He clawed about and found another yuckmawly. Holding it gently in his front claw, he began singing to it.

As Piko watched, the yuckmawly went soft and started to melt. Titanium Tim shouted to make it freeze still, but instead it shattered like glass. The lizard brushed the pieces off his claw.

"I try to sing them into perfect spheres, into balls," said Titanium Tim, "because they would be gorgeous with all their colors. I could decorate my other sculptures with them. The only problem is—" He clawed up another yuckmawly, held it close, and sang softly again. It promptly collapsed like a smashed egg. "They're too sensitive."

Piko thought the lizard focused too much on his failures. "But you can sculpt everything else, right? And you do it brilliantly! I'd love to see more of your work."

The lizard looked at Piko out of the corner of his eye. "Then will you go away?"

Piko agreed. Titanium Tim looked about suspiciously, then tugged at one of the mossy shapes. The moss pulled away. Beneath it was a sculpture shaped like a giant mushroom. He pulled the moss off more of the shapes. One statue looked like a turtle. Another resembled a spiral shell. Still another looked like the lizard himself — perhaps a self-portrait.

"They're beautiful! Why do you cover them with moss?"

"To protect them," said Titanium Tim. "The moss deadens all sound. Without it, any singing could change their shape. Birds are the worst." He looked up at the sky.

Piko reached out a webbed foot to feel one of the sculptures. It was smooth and hard. "What are they made of?"

"Clang root," said Titanium Tim. He slapped one with a claw. It clanged.

"It must be really strong," said Piko.

"And hollow," said Titanium Tim.

Piko now understood why Rosetta had directed him here. These would make wonderful spaceships! He looked at one after another until at last he stopped before a sculpture that was long and narrow, with fins. It looked very much like a spaceship!

"Oh, I love this one! It's your best one," he said. "Titanium Tim, I very much want this sculpture, and I'd be willing to give you some very tasty fish for it."

The lizard thought a moment. "Fresh fish?"

"The freshest," said Piko, although he had no idea how he would deliver them. "Oh, but the sculpture will need a door. I need to get in and out. And it has to be airtight."

The lizard thought some more. "I'll add a door you can open and close with a simple command, and it will always seal airtight. I can have it ready tomorrow at noon — if you will bring me 12 fresh fish."

"Twelve? Okay. But remember. It has to be airtight."

Chapter 6

A Plan to
Deliver Fresh Fish

That evening, Piko and his friends met with Slim the snail to give him their reports.

"Let's keep this short," said Slim. "I need to get somewhere. I don't have all day for this."

"Couldn't you keep moving while we talk?" asked Duffy the giraffe. He understood how long it takes for snails to get anywhere.

"No, I can't," said Slim. "I have to think with my whole brain to create slime. And without slime, I can't move. So, give me your reports quickly so I can be on my way."

Jeb reported that his pelican friends were telling everyone on the island about the launch. Meanwhile, Duffy had met with some weaver birds deep in the forest. They had agreed to weave a strong parachute in exchange for 12 pearls.

"Twelve pearls!" exclaimed Woobie. "They are thieves, that's what they are!"

As for Jelly and Buster, they were still looking for a way to keep the spaceship cool while it sat on the geyser.

When it was Piko's turn, he explained his problem. "There's a lizard in the bog with the perfect spaceship. He'll give it to me tomorrow at noon, but I have to bring him 12 fresh fish. Only it's too far for me to carry them without their rotting before I get there."

Slim moved his eyestalks, looking about. "Jeb, you can help."

Jeb the pelican was dozing on Buster's back. He jumped in surprise. "Me?"

"You can carry 12 fish in your pouch," said Slim. "Deliver them to the lizard tomorrow at noon."

"To the lizard in the bog?" cried Jeb. "But he hates birds! And he has a slingshot!"

"Land a safe distance away," said Slim. "You'll be fine."

"No, no. Sorry. Too dangerous."

Woobie tapped his claws together, thinking. "Do you like sea cucumbers?" he said.

"I love them!" squawked Jeb. "But they're too deep in the ocean for me to reach."

"Well, Piko will give you two sea cucumbers for your efforts — one before you deliver the fish and one after."

"I'll do it!" cried Jeb. "I'll do it I'll do it I'll do it!"

"One more thing," said Piko. "I can't carry the spaceship back by myself."

"I'll help you," said Buster, raising his rhinoceros horn high. "I like traveling. I love adventure!"

Slim ended the meeting. After everyone had left, Piko stepped close to the big snail, who had started moving again. "Slim?"

Slim stopped, looking the tiniest bit annoyed. "I really need to get somewhere, Piko."

"Just a quick question. I was wondering. Do you think it's dangerous, what I'm about to do?"

Slim's eyestalks twitched. "Dangerous? Oh, heavens no. No no no. What could be dangerous about hurtling straight up into space where there's no air, no gravity, there's nothing, just blackness and emptiness and, and—" He slowly tilted his blunt head and gently tapped Piko's wing with an antenna. "You'll be fine."

Chapter 7

Piko and Buster
Get Star Racer

The next morning, Piko made a side-trip to the ocean. He dove all the way to the bottom and picked two sea cucumbers from among the black coral. Back home, he found Jeb perched on Crazy Stump in the village center.

"Here you go, Jeb." He batted a sea cucumber into the air.

Jeb opened his beak and caught it in his pouch, then flipped it down his throat. "Ummm, ummm. Thanks, Piko!"

"Remember to deliver 12 fish at noon," he said. "They have to be very fresh."

"Don't worry, I will." Jeb eyed the other sea cucumber hungrily. "Oh, give me the other one now, Piko. Please? I'm starving. I promise I'll deliver. You can trust me."

Piko didn't want the pelican to be hungry, so he tossed Jeb the other sea cucumber.

"Thanks, Piko. You're the greatest!" said Jeb, flapping his wings and taking off into the sky.

Piko and Buster set off for the bog to pick up the Star Racer. At the bridge, the Blue Grumble confronted them, working his abacus. "Four," he said.

Piko had given him two blueberries coming back the last time, so four was certainly correct. But he wasn't sure it was fair to the troll.

"Are you sure that's okay?" asked Piko. "My friend Buster is very big, so if you need to charge more—"

"Four," said the troll.

"You are so generous! Thank you!"

Once they gave him four blueberries, the Blue Grumble kicked the trunk of the tree, and once more it ribboned with a shudder across the gulch. As Piko and Buster started across, the bridge swayed mightily. Buster was so big that his body hung over the sides. Halfway across, Buster turned talkative.

"Piko, why do you suppose they call it Don't Look Down Gulch? I've always wondered about that."

Piko clamped his beak tight and refused to answer. If he explained it to Buster, Buster was sure to look down, and then they would be lost.

Finally they made it across, and soon they were deep in the bog. As they approached Titanium Tim's place, Piko told Buster to stop.

"You stay back here out of sight. You're big, and you might frighten him."

Buster was not glad about this, but he said, "Okay."

Titanium Tim had the sculpture out and ready for Piko. But he also had other sculptures out that Piko had not seen. Many were bigger and fancier than the one he had chosen. Piko wandered among them, amazed.

Suddenly, Buster jumped from his hiding place. He was too excited to stay hidden. "Oh, look at that one with fins and wings!" he cried. He pointed his horn at the one Piko was admiring most.

Titanium Tim leaped with fright at the sight of Buster. But Piko told him Buster was a friend. Tim relaxed. "Only 30 fresh fish for that one," he said.

Piko walked around it again and again. It had wings and fins and was very beautiful.

"You should get it," said Buster. "It will fly so much better!"

But Piko realized how useless wings and fins would be. After all, he wouldn't really be flying. The geyser would just shoot him straight up into space. Up there he would float, not fly, because there was no air. So wings and fins were not really needed. Besides, Jeb's pelican pouch couldn't hold 30 fish.

"I better stick with my first choice," said Piko.

Tim nodded and crawled over to the sculpture Piko had chosen first. He showed how the door worked. "To open it, say, 'Clang root knot, open wide.' To close it, say, 'Clang root knot, close tight.'" Piko tried it, and the door opened and closed to these commands.

"So, what about those fresh fish?" asked the lizard.

Piko looked about in the sky and finally spotted Jeb. "Here they come now!"

"A bird," whined Titanium Tim, grabbing up his slingshot.

"No, he's a friend! And he can't sing!"

Piko ran to where Jeb had landed, a safe distance away. "Good timing, Jeb. Did you fly straight and fast?"

"Straight as an arrow. Fast as a bat. But Piko—"

"No time to talk! Give me the fish. Come on, Jeb. I need the fish now."

But when Jeb emptied his pouch, Piko found himself looking at a bunch of flowers.

"Aren't they pretty?" said Jeb. "I found you the prettiest flowers I could."

"But what about the fish!" exclaimed Piko. "You were supposed to deliver fish!"

"I got hungry," said Jeb. "Don't you like the flowers?"

"Go! Go away!" snapped Piko. "Why did I ever trust you?"

Piko walked back to the lizard and apologized. "Sorry I wasted your time, Titanium Tim. I don't have the fish after all."

"You shouldn't have trusted a bird," said Tim. "They're nothing but trouble."

Piko tucked his wings tighter against his sides. Giving the spaceship a last look, he motioned to Buster, and they started to leave. Then Piko stepped on something dry and crinkly. He looked down. It was a yuckmawly. He pulled it from the soggy ground. Though colorful, it was all twisted and lumpy. How ugly it was!

He held it close and tried singing softly to it. The yuckmawly wobbled uncertainly, then its shape began to grow round. Piko shouted to freeze it, but it shattered instead. Titanium Tim was right. Yuckmawlies were impossible to sculpt. Suddenly, he had an idea.

"Titanium Tim!" he called, rushing back to the lizard. "If you'll let me have that sculpture right now, I'll give you

three perfectly round yuckmawlies, just like you've been trying to make."

"Show me," said Tim.

"I can't do it right now," said Piko, "but I'll have them for you at the end of the month."

Titanium Tim shook his head. "You failed to deliver the fish. Why should I trust you now?"

Piko looked down in shame. He kicked at the bog underfoot. "I don't suppose you should." Then he looked up, his eyes brightening. "But honest, I'll deliver this time. And if I don't, I'll come work for you for a whole month. I'll clean your place, do chores, gather clang roots for you, anything."

"I don't know . . . "

"Okay, five yuckmawlies," said Piko. "I'll deliver five yuckmawlies. And if I fail, I'll be your servant for a month."

Titanium Tim rubbed his snout. "Okay. A deal. But I'm curious. Why are you so determined to have this sculpture?"

Piko knew he shouldn't tell, but he couldn't help himself. "You're looking at Star Racer! It's my spaceship! I'm going to ride it into space!"

Titanium Tim looked frightened. "So that's why it must be airtight!" he said. "Listen, Piko, when you're up there in space, no singing. You mustn't sing, or your Star Racer will turn soft. It will melt about you, and who knows what will happen."

Piko thought about this. "Sometimes when I'm happy I just start singing and don't even know it."

"You mustn't sing," said Titanium Tim. "Up there in space, you mustn't sing." He covered the sculpture in moss. "Keep it covered like this while you're moving it," he said. "Otherwise, anyone who sings nearby could damage it. Birds are the worst. That's why I hate birds." Suddenly the lizard eyed Piko suspiciously. "Say, you're not a bird, are you?"

Piko laughed nervously, then gave his tiny wings a lame flap. "Hah, does it look like I could fly?"

Titanium Tim relaxed. "Take care, Piko. You are very brave to be going into space."

Buster used his rhinoceros horn to carefully nudge Star Racer onto his big back. Piko tied it there using rope he had brought along. Then they set off. When they reached Don't Look Down Gulch, Piko picked eight blueberries and gave them to the Blue Grumble. The bridge swayed even more than before, and Buster kept asking why they called it Don't Look Down Gulch. But soon they were safely across with Star Racer and on their way.

Chapter 8

Gia the Whale

W here are we going?" asked Buster after they had walked a while. "This isn't the way home."

"I promised Rosetta I would test Star Racer in the ocean," said Piko. "We need to make certain it's airtight. So that's what we're going to do."

But when they reached the ocean, Piko didn't know how to do the test. "We need to hold Star Racer under the water to see if it leaks," he told Buster. "Can you hold it under?"

"Me? No, I'm not big enough. And I hate water. But look out there! See that spout? It's Gia the whale! I'll bet she would help."

Piko spotted Gia far out in the ocean and sighed. "I can't ask her for a favor."

"Why not?"

"Because the whales are already doing us penguins a huge favor. They protect us from the sharks. If sharks enter our waters, the whales drive them away. We owe them so much already that I dare not ask them for another favor. I would be embarrassed."

Buster had lost interest and was studying seashells in the sand.

Suddenly Piko had an idea. "What if we tricked Gia into helping? That wouldn't be the same thing, right? Right, Buster?"

"Huh? Oh, yeah, right."

"Here's what we're going to do. I'll climb into Star Racer and seal the door. When I'm ready, I'll knock three times.Then you roll me down to water's edge and shout, 'Hello, Gia!' When she blows her spout, you tell her, 'I bet you can't hold this thing under water for five minutes.' Then you kick me into the water. Okay?"

Buster was now watching little crabs crawling in the sand. "See these crabs, Piko? Don't they look like they're wearing uniforms? I wish I had a uniform."

"Buster! Are you listening?"

"Yeah, yeah. Tell the whale to hold you underwater as long as she can."

"No! Just for five minutes!"

"They really do look like uniforms," said Buster, lowering his nose to the sand for a closer look at the crabs.

"Buster! Did you hear what I just said?"

"Of course I heard you. I'm not deaf."

Piko sighed. Then he said, "Clang root knot, open wide," to open the door. Once inside, he said, "Clang root knot, close tight," and the door closed. He knocked three times to let Buster know he was ready. Nothing happened. He knocked harder three more times. He was about to open the door to see what was wrong when Star Racer began to roll. Finally!

He tumbled head over heels as Buster rolled him toward the water. Then he slammed into the wall as Buster butted him out into the ocean. Ouch! As Star Racer tossed and turned and plunged, Piko wished he had put some padding inside. He was getting all banged up! Where was his cap? He'd lost his cap! Spotting it tumbling past, he grabbed it and tugged it back on. He could see he was going to need a good cushion for blast-off.

Several minutes went by. Then he was rolling again. At last all was still. When he heard three knocks from outside, he spoke the command that opened the door. He rolled out onto the sand, very dizzy.

"See?" called Gia from the shallows, spouting proudly. "I held it under for five minutes. Now what do you say?"

"You did it!" Piko whispered to Buster. "And Star Racer passed as well! She's airtight. There's not a drop of water inside!" Piko felt a flicker of guilt at having tricked Gia. If only he could thank her. But then he'd have to admit he had tricked her, and she might not like that.

As Piko and Buster celebrated the moment, Rosetta dropped from the sky and landed on Star Racer.

"Hi, Piko. How's the project going? Have you made any progress?"

"Yes!" laughed Piko. "You're sitting on it. You're sitting on Star Racer!"

Rosetta flapped softly into the air, surprised.

"And it's airtight," said Piko. "I tested it in the ocean like you wanted me to, and not a drop of water got in."

"That's very good," said Rosetta. She fluttered around Star Racer, then landed on top of it again. "Piko, when you're up there in space, how will you look out?"

"What?" Piko felt incredibly foolish. "No! Oh no! Oh dear, oh dear, oh dear. I'll be in the dark up there, unable to see anything."

"Oh, Piko," sighed Rosetta. "You really must think things through before starting."

"I didn't think things through at all, did I?" wailed Piko. "You warned me, and I didn't pay attention. And now I've failed."

"You only fail if you stop trying," said Rosetta.

"But I'll have to start all over!"

"Is that really so bad? Why don't you take Star Racer back to the lizard. Ask if he can add a window. But remember, it has to be airtight."

Chapter 9

An Upgrade
to Calico Clangroot

Sixteen," said the Blue Grumble after working the abacus. Once Piko paid him, the troll kicked the tree, and it ribboned across the gulch. Piko and Buster crossed Don't Look down Gulch again, this time hauling Star Racer after them. They traveled deep into the bog and eventually came to the lizard's lair.

"Hi, Titanium Tim," said Piko, feeling embarrassed. "Uh, we ran into a problem. I was wondering if you could add a window."

Titanium Tim looked annoyed. "We had a deal, Piko."

"I know, but I made a mistake. I didn't think ahead. I'll need a window if I'm to see anything up in space. If you add a window, I'll give you seven perfectly round yuckmawlies instead of five."

Titanium Tim sighed. "I can't add a window to this one. I'd have to make a new one. There's a place in the bog where calico clang root grows. It's red, orange, green, and clear. I could sculpt one of those. The clear areas would work as windows. And I could add a door, same as before."

"I'd really appreciate it, Titanium Tim."

"Still, it's a lot of work," he said. "I'd be starting over from scratch, and doing more."

Piko swallowed hard and did some math in his head. "I'll give you 10 perfectly round yuckmawlies for it."

Slowly the lizard nodded. "Okay, but I'll need five days to complete it. Calico clang root is tricky to shape."

"Great!" cried Piko. "You are the best!" He wanted to hug the lizard, but knew the lizard was much too shy to appreciate it. Agreeing to come back in five days, Piko and Buster headed back. At the bridge, they picked 32 blueberries and gave them to the troll.

Chapter 10

Buster Feels Cheated

Piko and his friends met with Slim to give him an update on their progress. Slim had traveled only fifty feet from where he had been on the day they started the project.

"Sadly," said Woobie the hedgehog, "the first order of business is Jeb. He failed to deliver fresh fish as promised."

Jeb, who was dozing on top of Jelly's head, came fully awake. He flapped his wings in surprise. "How do you know that?"

Buster's stomach started to growl.

"You told on me!" squawked Jeb, glaring at Buster. "Your stomach always growls when you're hiding something. Why did you tell on me?"

"This isn't about Buster," said Slim. "It's about you, Jeb. You promised to deliver fresh fish, and you didn't."

Jeb tucked his beak shamefully under a wing. "I meant to. I did. But I got hungry."

Slim looked at Piko. "Piko? Did you give Jeb both sea cucumbers at the start?"

Piko nodded. "He was so hungry, and I didn't think it would matter."

Woobie shook his head. "Doesn't anyone around here have any sense? Piko, don't pay in full until you get the goods. You rewarded Jeb too soon."

"Well, we all have to keep our promises," said Slim. "Otherwise, this project will never get off the ground." Slim turned to Jeb. "I'm afraid some discipline is called for. Woobie?"

Woobie jotted in his notebook. "Jeb can't fish in the village pond for a month."

"But then I'll have to fly all the way to the ocean!"

"You heard Woobie," said Slim. "We've wasted enough time on this. Now I want updates from everyone."

Duffy reported that the weaver birds were almost done with the parachute, but they now wanted an additional five pearls.

"Thieves!" cried Woobie. "How dare they change the deal! We won't pay! Not a pearl more!"

"Settle down, Woobie," said Slim. "Unfortunately, we need that parachute. So we'll have to pay the extra pearls. Okay?"

Still grumbling, Woobie took five pearls from the project fund and gave them to Duffy to give to the weaver birds.

"Jelly, you're next," said Slim. "Did you figure out how we'll keep Star Racer from overheating while it sits on the geyser?"

Jelly nodded. "I found a flat rock that we can put on the geyser. We'll then set Star Racer on the rock. The rock will soak up most of the heat."

"Good," said Slim. He turned his eyestalks to Piko. "Which brings us to Star Racer. None of this will work if we don't have a spaceship. Piko, is there any chance we can still work a deal with that lizard?"

Piko gave a clever grin. "I already did. In five days, I'm picking up Star Racer!"

Slim was pleased with the news, but Woobie was suspicious. "Piko?" said Woobie. "Why would the lizard give you a spaceship if you haven't given him any fish?"

"I figured out something else he wants," said Piko. "I promised to deliver it at the end of the month."

"I'll need to know what it is," said Woobie, opening his notebook. "We need to keep track of every deal."

But Piko didn't want to tell anyone about his plan with the yuckmawlies. "I've got it under control," he insisted. "I'll have Star Racer in five days."

"We're going to trust you on this, Piko," said Slim. "So you better know what you're doing. Any other business?"

"Oh, a cushion!" said Piko, remembering how banged up he'd got while testing the first Star Racer in the ocean.

"I'm going to need a cushion. A really good cushion for the blast-off — or it's going to hurt. A lot."

"Of course," said Slim. "Why didn't I think of that?" He looked about. "Jelly, could you look into finding Piko a cushion?"

"I'll find him the best cushion there is," said Jelly.

After the meeting, Piko invited everyone to his toadstool hut for a feast. Everyone but Slim, who couldn't have got there anytime soon. Besides, Slim was still headed somewhere.

The menu included everyone's favorite food. There were sardines for Piko, mackerel for Jeb, cattails for Buster, and fig leaves for Duffy. Jelly the elephant even brought her famous bumble pudding, much to everyone's delight.

"This is delicious," said Jeb, clacking mackerel juice from his beak.

"Piko," said Woobie, still worried, "this deal you have with the lizard. Are you sure you know what you're doing?"

Piko nodded. "He'll get what I promised him. And he'll give me Star Racer in five days."

The stump tables were now bare, and everyone was full and relaxing.

"Buster," Jelly asked, "are you feeling okay?"

Buster had been unusually quiet. He had hardly touched his bale of cattails, and he held his rhinoceros horn very high, gazing up at the sky.

"I want to go along," he said. "I want to go into space too."

"Come on, Buster," said Piko. "You couldn't possibly fit into Star Racer."

"I'll go on a diet," Buster said.

"You're a rhino, Buster," Duffy reminded him. "You're just too big!"

"The geyser was my idea!" snapped Buster, whipping his big horn about in the air. "I figured out how to use it. And you stole my idea!"

"Please, Buster," said Piko.

Buster stuck out his lower lip in a pout. "You can't use Golly Geyser. I won't let you. Go find your own geyser." He stomped off.

All the delicious food in Piko's stomach turned sour. He felt beaten. Everyone around him also looked miserable.

"Well, that's that," said Jelly. "Without that geyser, we can't launch."

"I'll find another geyser," snapped Piko. "If Buster wants to be like that, I'll find a geyser of my own. Because I'm going into space. I'm going!"

Chapter 11

Very Expensive Toll

Piko used maps of Robin Island to locate other geysers. But when he traveled to those spots, the geyser was always too small.

Finding another geyser wasn't the only problem. The Blue Grumble was becoming difficult, too. He always doubled the number of blueberries from the last time, as he said he would do. At first, it didn't matter much, the difference between two blueberries or four. But Piko had crossed the bridge many times in his search, and the toll had climbed from 64 blueberries to 128, to 256, to 512, and now, suddenly—

"1,024," said the Blue Grumble after consulting the abacus.

Piko looked at the surrounding bushes. They were all picked clean. It would take him days to find 1,024 berries! And coming back it would be 2,048! This had become way too expensive.

"Couldn't you charge me less?" he asked the Blue Grumble. "You let me cross that first time for just one blueberry. How about if I pick you a whole bucket? That's way more than what I paid the first time."

The troll listened, then reworked the abacus. "2,048," he said.

Piko tried again. "Haven't I been a good customer? Couldn't you give me a better deal?"

The troll nodded, banged the abacus beads about, and announced, "4,096."

Piko walked off, feeling angry. As he kicked at pebbles, a bird settled on a branch nearby.

"Hi, Piko. How is the project?"

He looked up, surprised. He didn't recognize Rosetta at first because she wasn't all red as usual. She had dusted her wings with a blue powder, tucked a peacock feather in her tail, and fixed colorful feathers to her crest.

"I'm headed to a wedding," said Rosetta. "That's why I'm dressed up, and why I can't stay long. But you seemed so sad that I decided to stop."

Piko told her of his troubles — both with the Blue Grumble and with Buster.

"Don't make Buster your enemy," said Rosetta. "He's still your friend. He just feels left out. Maybe instead of looking for another geyser, you should try to make up with him." Rosetta glanced up at the sun. "Look, I'm late. But here's what you need to do. See that pond over there? Swim in it for an hour."

"But I don't have an hour to spare!"

"Trust me, Piko. Swim around for an hour and relax. Think of nothing. When you're done, you'll have an idea."

"How can I have an idea if I don't think?"

"The best ideas come when you're not trying."

"Who's getting married?" Piko thought to ask.

Now it was Rosetta's turn to look sad. "One of my daughters. She's marrying a blue jay. Can you believe it? A blue jay. What's this world coming to?"

As Rosetta flew off, Piko realized he wasn't the only one with troubles. Then with a sigh, he walked over to the pond, jumped in, and began to swim. It wasn't easy clearing his mind. Time and again he caught himself thinking. But each time he made an effort to stop.

After an hour he climbed from the pond.

He had an idea!

Chapter 12

Fergie Funnelby
and Her Funnel Web

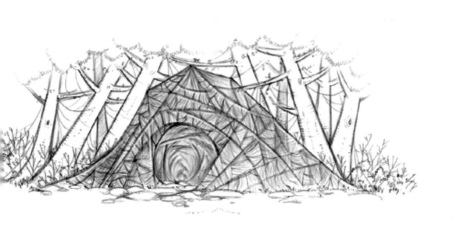

Piko stopped before the funnel spider web that stretched across Don't Look Down Gulch. Its near end was large enough to swallow Buster, while its far end was the tiniest speck of light. It was like a curving tunnel that got ever smaller, all spun of spider silk. Yes, he might be able to cross this way, if he could get past the gigantic spider lurking just within.

"Hi, Fergie Funnelby," he called. "You have a most beautiful web!"

"Flattery is yummy," said Fergie, tapping her eight legs on strands of web, "but it won't get you through, because I see in you a very fine stew."

"Yummy!" came a chorus from above.

Piko looked up and saw hundreds of baby spiders in the top of the funnel. He took a step back.

"Nothing personal," said Fergie, looking at him with her tiny black eyes. "It's just who I am and what I do."

"Understood," said Piko. "Still, it's very beautiful."

"Not like a butterfly," said Fergie, getting ready to lasso some butterflies fluttering close by. But they stayed just out of reach. "See how they taunt me with their colors? That's why I love eating butterflies. They laugh at my dull funnel web, that's what they do."

Piko walked away, for he had another idea. Ever since the swim, he had been full of ideas. Rosetta had been right. He just needed to relax and let the ideas come to him.

Back at the bridge, Piko searched through the bushes, picking the few blueberries he could find.

"8,192," said the Blue Grumble, working his abacus.

"Sorry," said Piko. "These aren't for you."

The troll, looking troubled, repeated less certainly, "16,384."

"Ta ta," said Piko, leaving.

Back at the funnel web, Piko tossed several blueberries into the web around Fergie. "Eat some of these."

"Fruit is for bats!" said Fergie. "It's bugs that I catch."

"Oh, give it a try. Eat five. Please. There's a reason."

Slowly Fergie tried them, going, "Bleah!" each time.

"Bleah!" chorused her babies in the web up above.

"Now try spinning something."

Reluctantly Fergie did so, then turned around in surprise. "Blue! I'm spinning blue, woo-hoo!"

"I can get you some other colors too, if you like."

"Yippee yoo-hoo, come on through, bringer of blue, I won't eat you!"

"We won't eat you!" repeated the babies, except one who said, "Bleah!" The other babies quickly pounced on him.

Piko stepped onto the web. It bounced and sagged, far worse than the tree bridge. It took all his courage to go forward. He passed by Fergie, then ducked under the babies. After a few minutes, he didn't stumble so much. He walked on, disliking the way the funnel kept narrowing. He would never be able to fit Star Racer through the narrow opening at the far end. Still, if his plan worked, he wouldn't have to. At last he squeezed through the web's small opening, and stepped out on the far side of Don't Look Down Gulch.

He walked along the edge of the gulch until he spotted the Blue Grumble's tree on the far side. The Blue Grumble was resting against it.

"Hi, Blue Grumble!" he called across Don't Look Down Gulch.

The troll stood up and picked up his abacus. He gazed across at Piko, looking puzzled. "32,768?" he said.

"I got a deal with Fergie Funnelby!" Piko called. "She's letting me use her funnel web for free, with a promise not to eat me!" He realized that Fergie's rhyming was catching.

"65,536," said the troll, reworking the abacus. "71,072." Then he knocked the abacus over and looked up. "50?"

Piko thought about it. "You mean 50 this time, 100 the next, 200 after that, then 400—"

"50, 50, 50," said the troll.

Piko thought for a minute.

"How about 20, 20, 20?"

"25, 25, 25?" pleaded the troll.

"A deal," called Piko.

Piko picked 25 blueberries as the tree ribboned toward him, and soon he was crossing the bridge. He traveled on to the ocean, where he found one of the crabs that looked like it was wearing a uniform. He took it back with him to Golly Geyser.

Chapter 13

Buster Has a
Change of Heart

It's one of those crabs from the ocean!" said Buster, leaning over to look.

"So it is," said Piko, having placed the crab where Buster was sure to notice it.

Buster watched closely as the crab crawled sideways. "Doesn't it have the nicest little uniform?"

"I bet you'd look good in it," Piko said.

"I'm too big," said Buster sadly.

"I bet we could make a big one for you," said Piko.

"Really?"

"I bet we could."

"Would you? Would you? You really would? You would?"

"Well, I'm really busy," said Piko. "I've got so many problems to work out. I need to find another geyser, that's the biggest problem right now. I keep looking—"

"You could use Golly Geyser!" said Buster, his small dark eyes suddenly bright. "If you make me a uniform, I'll let you use Golly Geyser!"

Piko pretended to think this over carefully. "And you'll guard my Star Racer?"

"Yes! I'll wear my uniform and march back and forth, back and forth, guarding Star Racer!"

Chapter 14

Another Deal with Fergie

When Piko returned to the funnel web, he saw that a whole section of the web was blue. It caught the sun's rays and shone like a dark blue sky. Dozens of butterflies fluttered just above, admiring it. Piko unloaded berries and fruits from a basket, all to be used as dyes.

"Yuck!" cried Fergie's babies upon seeing it all, but Fergie was very excited.

"Kind you are, stranger from afar," Fergie said.

"Could you do me one favor in return?" asked Piko.

"Anything within reason, if it's in season," said Fergie.

He pulled out the crab. "Could you make a uniform just like this?"

"A uniform I will spin, using colorful threads most thin!"

"Just one little problem," added Piko. "It has to be a hundred times bigger."

"A hundred times bigger!"

"It's for Buster."

"Buster in a uniform, odder than a unicorn!" said Fergie.

"If you do this, I'll bring you all kinds of colorful fruits every day for a month — more than you could ever spin."

Fergie thought that over. "Every day for three months," she said.

"A deal," said Piko, not wanting to push his luck.

"A deal!" cried the babies, except one who said, "32,768."

"How long will it take?" asked Piko.

"Two days spinning, to the end from beginning."

Piko thanked Fergie and said he would bring her only the most colorful of fruits. Then he dashed off, pleased at how well his plans were coming together.

Chapter 15

Star Racer with a View

Piko was glad to have Buster helping once more. On the day Star Racer was to be finished, they set off across Don't Look Down Gulch — paying the Blue Grumble 25 blueberries. They ventured on into the bog and were soon at Titanium Tim's place. The lizard had the new Star Racer all ready, and Piko and Buster circled it, amazed. Made of calico clang root, it had swirls of red, orange, green, and clear.

"It looks great!" cried Piko, touching a clear patch. "I'll be able to see out just fine."

Buster nudged the new Star Racer up onto his back, and Piko tied it there.

"Piko," said Titanium Tim, "once you're up there, how are you going to get safely down?"

"Oh, Slim the snail has other people working on that. It'll be fine. They're all very smart. Trust me, I'll make it back. And I'll deliver those perfectly round yuckmawlies on time."

Titanium Tim stepped close. Even though he looked away, he gently put a claw on Piko's shoulder. "Be careful,

Piko. And remember, when you're up there in space, don't sing. You must not sing a single note."

Piko said that he wouldn't. Then he and Buster headed off.

They crossed Don't Look Down Gulch, paying the troll 25 blueberries, then headed on toward Golly Geyser. Suddenly Rosetta appeared. She fluttered about Star Racer, then landed on a large mushroom.

"That is a marvelous spaceship," she said. "You'll be able to see so much. Did it test all right in the ocean?"

"Oh, I tested the first one." said Piko. "It would just be a waste of time testing this one."

Rosetta cocked her head. "Piko, isn't this a completely different spaceship? "

"Yes," said Piko. "But Tim does good work. If the first one worked, this one will, too."

Rosetta shrugged. "If I was going up in that thing, I'd want to make sure."

"You really want me to test it, don't you," Piko said. "If I did everything you wanted me to, I'd never make it into space!"

"I'm just speaking for myself," Rosetta said. "Of course, it's your decision."

Piko kicked at the grass. "Okay, I'll test it. I'll go to the ocean and test it. But it will work fine, you'll see."

"I'm sure it will," said Rosetta softly.

Piko knew Rosetta was right. Why did she always have to be right? But he shouldn't be angry with her for that. Then he remembered Rosetta's own problems. "How did that wedding go?"

Rosetta ruffled her feathers. "He's very nice, my daughter's new husband. For a blue jay, he's really very nice." Rosetta sighed. "I just can't stand his voice!"

"I suppose being nice is more important than having a nice voice," said Piko.

Rosetta cocked her head at him. "Now you're giving me good advice. Anyway, I'm glad you've decided to test your new Star Racer."

After Rosetta flew off, Piko and Buster headed for the ocean. Piko complained the whole way, muttering over and over, "What a waste of time!"

On the beach, he spotted Gia far out in the ocean. Piko hated to trick her again, but how else was he to test Star Racer? He told Buster the plan was the same as before — although Buster seemed more intent on telling the crabs that he would soon have a uniform just like theirs.

Piko commanded the door to open, then commanded it to close after he was inside. Through a window made of the clear clang root, he saw Buster shouting to Gia. Then Piko fell over as Buster nudged Star Racer toward the ocean.

Then he saw Buster charge. Piko tried to brace himself, but slammed into the wall as Buster butted Star Racer. Piko hit the wall again as the spaceship hit the water. He really hoped Jelly would find a good cushion soon.

Then Gia's big pink body swept over him and pressed Star Racer down into the depths. To Piko's horror, water gushed in all about him. What a disaster! He held his breath as Star Racer totally filled with water. He wasn't too worried, because he could hold his breath for an hour. But if this had happened up in space . . . it was too awful to think about.

Suddenly one of Gia's big blue eyes pressed against the window, looking in at him. Piko gave a tiny wave. Then he felt Star Racer being pushed toward shore. Soon the spaceship rested on the beach. Piko commanded the door to open and fell out in a rush of water.

"You okay, Piko?" asked Buster, nudging him with his horn.

"Fine, I'm fine," said Piko, sitting up. Then he saw Gia swimming about in the shallows.

"What were you doing?" asked Gia.

Piko explained about Star Racer, how he was going to ride it into space but first needed to test it in the ocean.

"You could have asked me to help," said Gia. "I really don't like being tricked."

"I'm sorry," said Piko. "My parents told me never to ask the whales for any favors. You keep the sharks away, and we owe you so much for that already."

"Please, I'd rather help than be tricked," said Gia. "Next time just ask me."

Piko did not want to take Star Racer back to Titanium Tim, but he simply had to. Back in the bog, Tim fixed the door.

"I'm ashamed I made a mistake," he said. "Now you need to bring me only six perfectly round yuckmawlies by the end of the month, instead of ten."

Piko thanked him. Then he and Buster set off with Star Racer. At the ocean, Gia helped test the spaceship, and this time it did not leak.

"Thanks, Gia," said Piko. "You are so kind. I wish I could do something for you. Is there anything you want? Anything you need?"

Gia thought a moment. "Maybe you could take something into space for me."

"Sure, if it isn't too big."

"It's just a tooth."

Piko looked at the six-inch teeth lining Gia's thin, flat, lower jaw. "Okay. Sure."

"One of them is a little loose," said Gia. She worked her jaw, then spouted water. A tooth flew out with the water and landed on the beach.

"Got it," said Piko, picking it up. "It's going on a long ride around the world with me. Then I'll bring it back to you."

"Thanks, Piko," said Gia. "I wish I could be there for the launch. But maybe I'll see you in the sky going up."

Chapter 16

Final Testing

Piko and the rest of the team tracked down Slim to give him the latest updates. Duffy showed everyone the parachute that the weaver birds had made. She waved it back and forth and showed how it filled with air. Then Jelly showed a big wad of moss she'd gathered that would serve as a cushion. Jeb reported that everyone on the island now knew of the coming launch, and he guessed that 30 animals might come.

"That leaves just one thing we still need," said Slim, turning to Piko.

With a smile, Piko stepped aside for the surprise he had planned. From behind a bush where he was hiding, Buster stepped out for all to see, with the new spaceship tied to his back.

"Behold, Star Racer!" cried Piko.

Slim stretched his eyestalks until they almost touched the spaceship. "Excellent. You have done well. Everyone has done well. We've got the spaceship, the cushion, the parachute, and the cooling plate. I knew you'd finish in plenty of time. I'm proud of all of you."

Piko beamed, happy as could be. "We could launch tomorrow. We've got everything we need."

Slim turned his head one way, then the other. He did so very slowly. Piko realized he was shaking his head "no."

"We'll launch at the end of the month, as planned," said Slim. "That's when we told everyone we would."

"But that's two more weeks!" said Piko. "And we're ready now."

"There's no need to rush," said Slim. "The geyser will still be there. The ship will still be ready. It wouldn't hurt to spend some time double-checking everything."

"This doesn't seem like good planning, Slim," said Duffy. "If you knew we'd be ready this soon, why did you set the launch date way out at the end of the month?"

Slim gave a long, deep sigh. "Okay, okay, I'll admit it. I set the launch date for the end of the month because that's how long it will take me to reach Golly Geyser."

"You mean—?" said Piko. "So that's where you've been headed all this time!"

"Yes, yes," said Slim. "I want to see this launch. I wouldn't miss it for anything in the world. It's selfish of me, I know. But that's the way it is. Which reminds me. I still have a long ways to go. No time to chat now."

The next morning, Piko headed for Golly Geyser to check on the spaceship. On the way, he spotted Jelly, who was placing the big wad of moss near a tree trunk.

"What are you doing with the cushion, Jelly?"

"I'm helping Rosetta. She found a very ripe grapefruit at the top of this tree. It's too heavy to carry down, and if she drops it, it will smash. So she wants to drop it on the cushion."

"Are you ready?" Rosetta called down from high above.

"Ready!" shouted Jelly.

Looking up into the tree, Piko spotted a tiny speck that grew ever bigger. It was the falling grapefruit. It hit the cushion dead center and splattered everywhere. Piko's eyes stung from grapefruit juice. He wiped at them with his wingtips.

"Oh dear, oh dear," said Jelly. "This moss doesn't make a very good cushion at all. That could have been you, Piko. Oh dear, oh dear. I need to find something much better."

After Jelly had wandered off, Rosetta flew down to land near the moss. She didn't look at all surprised.

"How did you know it wouldn't work?" asked Piko.

"I didn't," said Rosetta with a shrug, "but I knew it ought to be tested."

Piko nodded. "I suppose that means we should test the parachute, too."

"What a great idea! Actually, everything about the ship should be tested."

Duffy objected when told she should test the parachute. "But what's the point? The parachute is fine! The weaver birds did good work. It's strong. It's flexible. If I wave it in the air, it catches the wind and opens."

But Rosetta and Piko insisted that she take it to Sea Cliff, tie a big rock to it, and push it over the edge.

Grumbling, Duffy draped the parachute over her shoulder and headed off for a test.

Rosetta then turned to the penguin. "Piko, I want you to climb into Star Racer and close the door. I want you to stay inside for eight hours."

"Eight hours!"

"We should make sure you'll have enough air when you're up there."

At Golly Geyser, Piko brushed aside the protective moss and climbed inside Star Racer. After he commanded the door to close, Rosetta put the protective moss back.

Every few minutes, Rosetta brushed aside the moss to peek in at him. Piko made funny faces to tell her he was all right. Eight hours later, he came out.

"You were okay?" asked Rosetta.

"The air got a little stuffy, but I was fine."

Duffy had less success. She returned from Sea Cliff with a shredded parachute on her shoulder. "It tore," she said. "It wasn't nearly strong enough. It would have been a disaster for you, Piko."

Duffy went back to the weaver birds and asked them to make a stronger parachute. The birds agreed, but wanted 18 pearls for their efforts, because the tougher leaves would be harder to weave.

Meanwhile, Jelly looked for a better cushion. She tried mud, cattails, a giant lily pad, and bunches of leaves. But each time, when Rosetta knocked loose a grapefruit from the top of a tree, it would splatter when it hit the cushion.

"I didn't think all this testing was necessary," said Slim at another meeting with the team. "But I was wrong. There are more problems than I thought."

"We didn't have plenty of time after all," muttered Piko. "There's only two days left until the end of the month."

Slim kept the meeting short. After all, he still needed to reach the geyser. He told everyone to keep on testing, then resumed his crawl.

Later that day, Duffy galloped up to Piko. Draped about her long neck was a new parachute from the weaver birds. "I tested it at Sea Cliff," she said, excited. "I used a really heavy rock. It worked! It worked just fine!"

Soon after that, Jelly showed up with a large eagle's nest.

"I hope this works," she said, "because I paid an eagle five pearls for it."

She placed it near the base of a tree, then shouted to Jeb high above. Soon a grapefruit came sailing down. When it hit the eagle's nest, it splattered only a bit.

"That worked pretty well," said Piko, wiping grapefruit juice from his face.

"Only a little better," said Jelly. "It's still not very good."

"I'm sure it will be okay," said Piko. "Let's use it."

Finally, Slim finished his crawl to Golly Geyser. It had taken him 29 days. To celebrate, Jelly made a big batch of her bumble pudding. As they ate, they talked about the launch.

"Tomorrow's the big day," said Duffy. "And we did it! We're all ready."

"Not entirely," mumbled Jelly. "I never found a really good cushion."

"The eagle's nest will work fine," said Piko. "That grapefruit hardly splattered at all."

Jelly sighed, still not sure it would protect Piko.

Then Piko noticed Buster sneaking off. He was nudging a big bowl of bumble pudding along the ground, using his horn.

"What are you doing, Buster?" asked Piko. "I didn't think you liked bumble pudding."

Buster pushed the bowl up close to a tree. Then he looked upward and shouted, "Ready, Jeb!"

High above, Jeb the pelican knocked loose a grapefruit. It fell downward, getting bigger and bigger, and plopped into the big bowl of bumble pudding.

Piko stepped close and looked in the bowl. The top of the grapefruit stuck out above the pudding. He fished out the fruit and held it up for all to see. It was all in one piece – it hadn't broken at all!

"My bumble pudding!" exclaimed Jelly. "It makes the perfect cushion!"

"The solution was right under your nose this whole time," said Piko with a laugh. Everyone else laughed, too. Then they all had seconds of bumble pudding.

Chapter 17

Blastoff

Buster marched proudly back and forth in front of Golly Geyser, waving his rhinoceros horn in the air. He looked spiffy in his colorful uniform. Several crabs followed him about, mistaking him for their mother. He had placed the flat rock on top of Golly Geyser to soak up all the heat, then stood Star Racer on top of that. Otherwise, Star Racer would have got too hot inside before blast-off. Signs were posted everywhere, saying, "No Singing!" because Star Racer was no longer wrapped in moss.

Piko was surprised at how many animals had come out for the event. There was Slim, of course. And Woobie, Duffy, Jeb, and Jelly. Rosetta was there, too, sitting on a branch near Golly Geyser. She looked very worried. There were also lots of strangers. They had come from all parts of the island, and Woobie was kept busy taking two pearls from each of them.

"Look at that," said Duffy, gazing at the sky. "The weaver birds are flying around up there."

"Those crooks," grumbled Woobie. "First they overcharge us for the parachute. Then they fly around up there, watching the show for free."

"Relax, Woobie," said Slim. "There's not much we can do about it now. Let's just enjoy the launch."

Even the Blue Grumble showed up. Woobie asked him for two pearls, but all he had was 25 blueberries. With a sigh, Woobie accepted them as payment.

"Well, this is it," said Piko, stepping forward.

Jelly wrapped her elephant trunk around Piko's waist and lifted him up to the door. He could feel the heat from the flat rock. He waved to everyone as they called out their goodbyes. Then he commanded the door to open, slipped inside, and commanded the door to shut.

Now he just had to wait. There was no way to know when the geyser would blow. Even with the flat rock underneath, it was getting hot inside Star Racer. He was glad he had brought lots of water. He looked at the tub of bumble pudding he would climb into when the ground began to shake. He shuddered. It looked yucky. Folded neatly beside the tub was the parachute. The ends of its cords were tied to knobs in the clang root walls. Next to the parachute was a sack filled with those ugly yuckmawlies, as well as Gia's tooth.

He looked out a window at everyone gathered around. He still couldn't believe how many people had come. He counted at least 50. At two pearls each, that would be plenty to pay everyone back, and then some.

In the shadows he spotted Titanium Tim. Even he had come, though he stayed out of sight so no one would look at him. The lizard was very shy. Piko gave him a little wave and smiled.

Suddenly the ground rumbled, and Piko jumped into the tub of pudding. He jiggled about in it, feeling icky. Still, it felt like a mother's hug, and it would protect him. He tried to stay calm, but he couldn't. He was very afraid. What if Golly Geyser just exploded the spaceship? The rumbling grew worse. Then all at once a giant hand slapped down hard on every part of his body — or at least that's what it felt like. As he sank deep into the pudding, he saw clouds speeding past all around. He was shooting straight up at tremendous speed!

Chapter 18

Space

Piko floated about, bumping into the clang root walls of his ship. He flapped his stubby wings, and to his surprise that helped.

"I'm flying! I'm flying!" he cried. Although to be truthful, everything was flying, even the pudding. It rose from the tub in blobs that floated about like clouds. He dodged them, then grabbed his cap as it floated by. He tugged it tightly back on his head. Looking out a clear area of the wall, he saw night. It was the blackest night he had ever seen. But there were stars, too, brighter than he had ever seen them. He wished he could travel to a star. But not this time. This time he would just orbit the world – just sail around it once – then go back down.

He looked down at the world, so like a marble, with clouds and ocean and a small island. Robin Island! All his friends were there! He watched it move away as the world slowly turned, and now he saw strange new lands below he wished he could explore.

When a sack bumped into him and floated away, Piko remembered his promise to Titanium Tim. He grabbed the sack and opened it. Gia's large whale tooth floated out. He pulled out seven yuckmawlies. He had

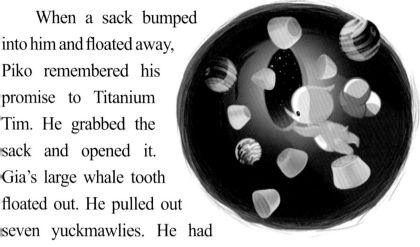

brought one extra, just in case. He remembered Titanium Tim's warning that he mustn't sing while up in space because the clang root would melt. But he would keep his voice down. He would sing very, very quietly.

Holding a yuckmawly close, he sang softly to it. Slowly it turned soft. Just as he had guessed, up here there was no gravity to flatten it out. Without gravity, it expanded evenly, becoming a perfectly round ball. He made a sharp chirp noise, and it froze. A perfect sphere! He did the others in the same way. As he sang softly to the last one, he looked up and stopped in alarm. Star Racer was changing shape! The calico clang root window was melting, bending inward here, bulging outward there. He had sung too loud! He shouted to freeze the last clang root, then waited. If there was a leak, all the air would be sucked out, and he wouldn't be able to breathe. He would die!

How careless of him, he thought. Rosetta and Titanium Tim would both scold him if they knew what he had done. He gathered up the seven yuckmawlies, and the whale tooth, and put them back in the sack. Afraid they might break, he scooped bumble pudding from the air and stuffed it inside the sack, too.

Star Racer began to shake as if a strong wind were blowing outside. He was re-entering the atmosphere. Soon the ship would be caught by gravity and start falling. He looked down out of a clang root window, trying to see where he would land. A small island was just coming into view.

Chapter 19

Return to Robin Island

As Star Racer tumbled straight down, Piko commanded the door to open. As it did, he squeezed tight against the wall and gripped his cap with his wingtips. A fierce wind whipped into the spaceship, knocking everything about. He waited for the parachute to be sucked out, where it would fill with air and bring Star Racer to a soft landing. But the parachute didn't move. The clang root had melted around it, and it was stuck to the wall! He knew he couldn't stay in Star Racer, or he would be crushed when it hit the ground. He had no choice but to abandon ship.

"Goodbye, Star Racer," he shouted. Then he jumped out, dragging the sack of perfectly round yuckmawlies after him. Maybe he could dive into the ocean. He had dove from cliffs into the ocean before. But this was a thousand times higher. As he fell, he looked straight down. The island! He was falling right toward Robin Island! If he hit the land, he would be killed!

He stretched out his stubby wings and tail as far as they would go. He craned his neck to point his beak at the ocean, then tilted his tail and his wings to follow his beak. He stretched to angle his fall toward the water.

The wind whipped past him. He squinted hard, trying to see. The island seemed to slowly move beneath him, and then he saw the ocean right below him. He wouldn't hit the land after all!

"I'm flying!" he cried. "This time I really am flying! I'm going to be okay!"

Letting go of the sack, he straightened his neck, pointed his beak straight down, and folded his wings. He hit the ocean so hard that he went straight down into the deep, dark depths. Black coral surrounded him. He had almost hit the bottom!

"Wow," he thought during the long swim to the surface. "That was fun!" He knew just how lucky he had been. At last his head broke through the water out into the air, and he took a deep breath. The sack was floating nearby. He grabbed it, afraid to look inside. What if they were all broken? But he did open the sack, scooped out the bumble pudding, and found all the perfectly round yuckmawlies to be just fine!

He then heard a spouting sound. It was Gia the whale!

"I saw you, Piko!" called Gia. "I saw you go up, and I saw you come down. Are you all right?"

"I'm all right," said Piko with a laugh. "I went up in space, floated around the world, and now I'm back and I'm fine! Oh, and I have something for you!" He pulled the large whale tooth from the sack, wiped off the pudding, and flipped it toward Gia.

Gia caught it in her mouth. "Thanks, Piko! I now have a tooth that's been up in outer space. I'll cherish it always!"

Then Piko heard loud cheers. Looking to shore, he saw all his friends there, ready to welcome him home.

Chapter 20

Celebration

It seemed only right to hold the celebration at Golly Geyser. After all, that's where it had all started. Besides, Slim was still there, and he wouldn't be getting anywhere else soon. And he simply had to be included.

First they held a short business meeting, just to get that out of the way.

"Where's Buster?" asked Slim.

"I saw him earlier today," said Duffy. "I don't know where he went."

"Well, we'll just have to start without him."

Woobie emptied a bag of pearls for all to see. "This is what we made from the launch. See? I told you you'd get your pearls back. I'm giving you twice as many pearls as you put in."

After Woobie had finished doing that, he put the remainder of the pearls back in the bag.

"Wait a second," said Jeb. "What about those pearls? Who gets them?"

Woobie lifted the bag. "This goes in the village fund."

"Village fund?" asked Duffy.

"For our next project," said Woobie.

"Next project?"

Slim nodded. "Whatever that might be."

They heard a loud clanging in the distance.

"What's that awful racket?" said Jelly, clamping her big ears tight against her sides.

Soon Buster came into view, butting something ahead of him.

"I found it near Don't Look Down Gulch," said Buster. "It was already banged up, by the way. I didn't make all these dents." He gave it one more butt so it came to rest near Piko.

"Star Racer!" cried Piko. He ran his wingtips over its surface. Indeed, it was terribly battered – both from his singing and from hitting the ground. He found it hard to believe he had ridden it into space, and that he had circled the world in it.

"Thanks, Buster," said Piko. "I really appreciate you finding it."

"We'll make it into a monument," said Slim. "It will serve as a memorial to what we accomplished."

"And to Piko's bravery," added Rosetta, fluttering down to land on a low branch.

They set up stump tables and decked them with every kind of food and delicious dessert. Jeb brought sardines,

Piko's favorite fish. Jelly brought even more of her bumble pudding than usual. Looking at the big bowl of pudding, Piko felt like he was about to launch again.

Everyone sang and danced and played silly games. Buster, still in his uniform, had taught several crabs to march, and now he led them back and forth, back and forth, in front of the geyser.

During the performance, Piko spotted Titanium Tim hiding in the bushes. Piko quietly slipped over to the lizard while everyone watched Buster and the crabs.

"Hi, Tim," Piko whispered. "I'm glad you came."

"I wanted to congratulate you," said Tim. "I was worried about you. It was very dangerous, going up into space like that."

"But you made me a wonderful ship," said Piko. "It kept me safe. Oh, and I have something for you!"

He pulled out the sack and handed it to Tim.

Tim looked inside and cried out, then clamped a claw over his mouth. He spoke in an excited whisper.

"Perfectly round yuckmawlies! I never thought you could do it! Thank you! Thank you!"

Then Piko heard the others calling his name. He hurried back to the party. Rosetta was now perched on a large mushroom in front of everyone.

"Piko, would you step forward?" she said.

"What's this all about?"

"Just step forward," said Jelly, nudging him with her trunk.

Piko stepped up beside Rosetta. Buster, Jeb, Woobie, Jelly, and Duffy all crowded around. Slim stretched out his eyestalks to get as close as he could to the group.

"Piko," said Rosetta, lifting a medal that was on a long string, "this is for your bravery and your spirit of adventure." She slipped it around Piko's neck. "I commend you as First Penguinaut!"

Piko looked down at the medal. It was shaped like Star Racer. Engraved in it was Piko's face. He looked shyly about as everyone cheered. Then he waved them silent.

"I couldn't have done it without all of you," he told them. "You helped so much. This is for all of us. We all earned this."

Just at that moment, Golly Geyser went off, and everyone turned to watch as steaming water shot 50 feet into the air. When it had quieted, Jeb flapped his wings impatiently.

"Enough talking," he said. "I'm starving."

Then the real feasting began.

M. K. Abraham lives with a small, deaf, calico cat in the San Francisco Bay Area, enjoys painting and sculpting as well as writing, and grows carnivorous plants and exotic vegetables in a backyard bog.

R.R. Jan has been drawing his dreams ever since he was a child. He lives with a playful rabbit that keeps him company while he works, though it is also hot-tempered and ever impatient for a walk.